Johnny Spicer's
LOS ANGELES NOIR

H. P. OLIVER

HPO Productions
8698 Elk Grove Boulevard, Suite 1-271
Elk Grove, California 95624

Cover art and book design by Steve Eitzen

Cover and title page photos © Water & Power Associates

Printed in the United States of America

ISBN-13: 978-0-9994150-2-3

MYSTERIES IN HISTORY

DEDICATION

To exist, noir evil requires the sort of darkness in which mankind's greed and inhumanity may grow and flourish uninhibited. This book is dedicated to the City of Los Angeles in recognition of its ability, imagined or otherwise, to provide just such an environment in the middle years of the 20th Century.

ACKNOWLEDGMENTS

The author gratefully acknowledges the writers in whose minds the noir film and literary genres were created. These included but were not limited to Raymond Chandler, Dashiell Hammett, Mickey Spillane, Ross Macdonald, James M. Cain, and Orson Welles.

PLEASE NOTE

This book occasionally refers to individuals and groups in terms that are considered disrespectful and inappropriate today. These terms, however, were commonly used during the noir era and are included here solely for the purpose of accurately depicting the attitudes and customs of the period.

INTRODUCTION

Who is Johnny Spicer?

Those who are familiar with my series of Johnny Spicer Capers know the answer to that question, but for the unenlightened, Spicer is a fictional character I created in the pulp fiction image of gumshoes who passed this way enroute to literary history. I speak of Sam Spade, Phillip Marlowe, and Mike Hammer, et al.

While Spicer might be likened to these classic fictional heroes, he is his own man, a unique conception in the same sense that Dashiell Hammett, Raymond Chandler, and Mickey Spillane were unique, yet endowed with the same sort of imaginations that sent them down the dark alleys of their minds in search of whodunnit.

A noticeable difference in Spicer's personality is found in his answer when asked if he carries a gun: "If I have to, but I prefer to talk the bad guys to death."

You will learn more about our hero in *Johnny Spicer's Los Angeles Noir*. That is unless you choose to use this book to prop up a short table leg. In that case, you will remain ignorant.

What is Noir?

"Noir" is French for black or dark. In the once colorful streets of Hollywood, the word was more often used to describe a film genre marked by moods of pessimism, fatalism, and a strong sense of menace.

Noir films reached their highest level of popularity

between 1944 and 1954. While writers, producers, and directors of the Orson Welles, Howard Hawks, and Billy Wilder ilks produced hundreds of noir films few saw, let alone remember today, some of those most highly praised by film critics (i.e. blathering idiots) are *Sunset Boulevard*, *Double Indemnity*, and *The Big Sleep*.

Did you notice the last book/film in this short list above was written by pulp fiction author Raymond Chandler, which brings us full circle. Tidy, don't you think?

What is Johnny Spicer's Los Angeles Noir?

This is a collection of observations from a cynic who makes his living rescuing clients set upon by evil while straying into the nether regions of the big city. Some are pushed there and some get there all on their own. Either way, Spicer rides to the rescue for a C-note per day and expenses.

What does Spicer observe? Life, death, and everything that happens in between. I think of Spicer's observations as single-sentence stories in a city where life goes on even when it doesn't.

In closing, I offer a word of caution. Noir, especially Johnny Spicer's brand of noir, is not intended for readers with weak stomachs or those lacking in imagination.

If, for example, you cannot imagine looking down the rock-steady barrel of a big revolver in the dainty hand of a gorgeous blonde doll with homicide in her cool blue eyes and revenge in her stone-cold heart, I suggest you trade this book in for *The Complete Works of Emily Dickinson*.

H. P. Oliver

JOHNNY SPICER'S
LOS ANGELES NOIR

Hollywood is just an illusion.
The only realities here are concrete
sidewalks and broken dreams.

The dame gave me a look she probably
thought was sexy. It had all the appeal
of a mashed potato sandwich.

There are more than a million people in LA, but you can still get lonely here . . . the worst kind of lonely.

If you meet a sweet, innocent gal in LA, don't bother askin' for her number . . . she's just passin' through.

They just called him "The Kid" because nobody knew his name. It'll make a short epitaph.

Any dame you'd look at twice
in this town is probably bad news.

Most times the victim of a blackmail scheme
is just as rotten as the blackmailer.
Otherwise, it wouldn't pay.

You can always tell a dame who is near the
end of her rope. She tries a little
too hard to please.

Hollywood has two big industries: movies and sin. Sin has the higher profit margin.

She was a redhead with enough class to make it big . . . only thing holding her back was the bullet hole between her eyes.

With this guy hate isn't just an emotion, it's a career.

She'd been a real looker before the good life caught up with her.

This town's full of kids who show up with dreams of fame and fortune. The lucky ones make it . . . back where they came from.

He was one of those mugs who does everything on the sly, and then whines 'cuz he never gets a break.

Sometimes I look at the faces of the people I
pass on the Boulevard, but not often.
Most of them just look lost.

He was just a little guy—not too bright
They called him Mousie. He swept up after
closing. He won't be sweeping up anymore.

This guy was a mean drunk.
You could see it in his eyes, he
was looking for someone to hurt.

The rain washed the concrete and scrubbed the air. Then the stars came out. As Hollywood nights go, this was a pipperoo.

A sixth sense makes my neck hair stand up when something's not right. Now they weren't just standing, they were running for cover.

Yeah, I carry heat when I have to, but I don't like to. I'd rather talk the bad guys to death.

I sat at my desk and listened to the city's night sounds. Tonight there were sirens—people in trouble or about to be.

My visitor had Bette Davis' eyes, Betty Grable's legs, and Jimmy Cagney's forty-five.

Sin might not have been born on the Sunset Strip, but it sure as hell grew up there.

Bouncy strains of Goodman drifted up from a jukebox across the Boulevard. Someone was having a swell time. It wasn't me.

She was a sweet young thing once, but that was ancient history. Now she was just another used-up dame nobody cared about.

My eyes crossed as he poked the pistol at my nose. I hoped he wouldn't pull the trigger. I sure didn't want to die looking like that.

She was just a kid, but she had a very grown
up gun that would make a very big hole
in me if she pulled the trigger.

They used to shoot movies in this town, but
most of the studios moved up to the valley
or went bust. Now they just shoot people.

I walked out on the pier hoping the roar of
the waves would drown out the blonde's
screams in my head. It didn't.

A lot of money slithers through this town and the punks hang around hoping some of it will rub off on them. It seldom does.

One more body wasn't gonna keep the homicide bulls from their beauty sleep, especially if it was my body.

LA's like a dame. Fall for her and she'll take everything you've got, and then break your heart just because she can.

He tried to forget. When that didn't work,
he tried an 80-proof eraser. That
worked a little better.

Trust you? Last time I trusted a dame she
pinched my wallet and tried to shoot me with
my own gun. I'm all outta trust, doll.

In this town cops are just crooks with
badges, only not as smart.

They used to grow stuff out on the Strip, but
they found out they could make
more money cultivating sin than alfalfa.

Sister Aimee came here to save us sinners.
Turned out she needed saving even
more than we did.

Just for laughs I took a stroll down the
Boulevard looking for something real that
wasn't tinsel and glitz. I didn't find it.

There were some decent folks living
in Hollywood once. They all
moved to Bakersfield.

In this town the cost of fame
and fortune is your soul. Star-struck
kids gladly pay the price.

Ann was a sweet kid when she
showed up to become a star.
Now she's 22 and looks 40.

From here you can take Route 66
to Chicago or Santa Monica.
Six of one, half a dozen of the other.

Most would-be starlets go home at night
smelling of the greasy burgers and stale
beer they hustled all day.

Helping good citizens out of trouble
on the dark side of town pays my rent,
but we're running low on good citizens.

In a city of two million faces seeing the same
face behind you twice in one day was
more than a coincidence.

They say trouble is where you find it, but
in my business trouble finds me.

People in other places have the
idea Hollywood is glamorous. Maybe it
is if you don't look too close.

In the early days Hollywood boarding houses put up signs saying, "No Actors." Now the actors own all the boarding houses.

Most movie folks aren't too bright. They do stupid things. That's why they need me.

The developers who created Hollywood all died and escaped the mess they made. Now the rest of us have to live with it.

After a while you learn the difference between cop sirens and ambulance sirens, a valuable skill in these parts.

They write happy songs about New York's Gay White Way. Music for the Sunset Strip is lowdown, blue and dirty.

They found her in one of the Angel's Flight funicular cars. Now she's an angel who's made her last flight.

I like Stan Kenton. He swings big and brassy. That fits LA, and if I get tired of the jazz, I can always look at June Christy.

I found the guy face down on the shore of Lake Hollywood. Now the lake has the same reputation as the town it was named for.

The carriage trade in this town likes the Coconut Grove. Look for guys like me in the Central Avenue jazz dives.

A guy out on the Boulevard was preaching
we should repent because the end is near.
I straightened my tie in case he was right.

For a good time they call Jilly. When the
good times turn bad they call Johnny.

They made an anti-drug film called "*Reefer
Madness.*" It convinced all the good kids
they were missin' out on something.

I always pause to glance down dark alleys.
It's good for business.

The LA River is 50 miles of dry concrete until
the winter floods come and drown all the
fools who come out to see the winter floods.

Hollywood was a religious town until actors
moved in. Now Flynn and Lucifer are next
door neighbors, and Lucifer is moving
to a better neighborhood.

Bogart? Yeah, I met him when I was workin'
a case for Jack Warner. He's an okay guy.
I mean Bogie. Warner's a louse.

First thing movie folks buy is a snazzy
car as long as the Santa Fe Super Chief.
Then they get drunk and crack it up.

One of Hollywood's first studios
was a closed down tavern They just
traded one bunch of sinners for another.

Family? Hah! Carl Laemmle's people have to raise chickens on his studio lot and Jack Warner steals from his brothers.

Hollywood is hard on dames. It uses 'em up and tosses 'em in the gutter like lipstick-smeared cigarette butts.

We move in different circles. She shops at Bullocks Wilshire and I shop at Sam's Army-Navy Surplus on Western.

Out on the Boulevard you've got sharpies with angles and citizens with gullibility. Think of me as an equalizer.

Both LA and New York are lousy with seagulls and pigeons. Both places are for the birds.

Guys who write detective stories make it sound exciting. What's exciting about broken-down dames and two-bit punks?

A few of my competitors hang out at a cop bar on Spring so they can hear what's new. I don't. Cops make me nervous.

She was a rarity in LA—a dame with Victorian morals and religious scruples. A snowball in hell had better odds.

He was a dapper little guy with a nifty Homberg, a trick walking stick, and shifty eyes.

It doesn't matter how many dead guys I see, I
just can't get past the idea they were
all alive once . . . like me.

At the turn of the century they
started calling it "smog." No matter the
name, it's still garbage like all our other trash.

Ya know how Santa Monica's Pleasure
Pier got built? They needed it to build their
raw sewage pipeline out into the ocean.

The first white guy who showed up here—a
padre—said you couldn't see anything
for all the smoke. Blame the Indians.

It was a stifling night. The open office
window let in two loud pops. Could've been
backfires. Could've been gunshots.

The dame in 314 at the Roosevelt
was havin' a bad night. Room service
forgot the ice and somebody slit her throat.

High-heel shoes are swell, but impractical if a
heel gets stuck in the fire escape. She
never thought to take them off.

I'm willing to pay a little extra for exotic
ambiance, but when a Martini costs a buck, I
get back on the boat for San Pedro.

The HOLLYWOODLAND sign?
I say leave it alone. It'll fall down in
a year or two and that'll be the end of it

Once LA tourists went to Ostrich farms. Now they go to Grauman's Chinese for footprints. The big birds were more fun.

It's 270 miles to Vegas—six hours on good tires. Just throw your money off the Santa Monica pier and be done with it.

Building a ghost town at Knott's Berry Farm? That's nuts! No one will drive clear down to Orange County for an amusement park!

Arroyo Seco Parkway—a fix for LA's traffic jams—is open. Folks can now drive 45 MPH for eight miles. Whoa, Nellie!

There are days when I think Hollywood is a damned strange place to live. The rest of the time I'm sure of it.

"Iron Man" Ardizzone? Yeah, I knew him. He ran the LA mob. His hobby was going to funerals. They threw him a nice one in 1931.

The Gilmore Station at Beverly and
Fairfax upped their price to 12-cents/gallon.
Horses may come back yet.

As a group, motion picture
people are insecure, overpaid, and
generally annoying. You can have 'em.

Beverly Hills folks are lousy neighbors, but
if you aren't lily-white and in the social
register, no need to worry about it.

Cops rousted John Wayne for tossing billiard balls at passing cars below his fifth floor window at the Hollywood Athletic Club. This town's no fun anymore.

Her big brown eyes were screaming "help" with a capital H.

He was a sucker for dames. If a blonde gave him a come-hither look, he came hither and woke up with an empty wallet.

Looking down on the city from Griffith
Observatory the streetlights make
orderly patterns that hide the chaos.

She stood on the hillside at Hollywood
Memorial and stared at a new headstone.
Moonlight made tears on her cheeks glisten.

Film Noir? That's just decent people paying
two bits to see how the other half lives.

Los Angeles is a living, breathing being. It can think and it can do. The only part it doesn't have is a heart.

Saw the new Warner Bros. musical last night. Keeler danced, Powell sang, and Jack Warner made another million.

We work to feed our families. Crime and government have the idea we should work to feed their families.

When facing a tough
decision, pick the hardest choice
to do. It's usually the right thing to do.

In this town what you don't
know may not hurt you, but what you
do know can and often does.

Chinatown, Korea Town, Japan
Town . . . Orientals like to keep some
distance between them and us. Smart folks.

The stiff had my card on him,
but someone changed it to read *Johnny
Spicer DeFective Agency.* Cute.

From 25 feet the dame
sparkled like Beverly Hills, but
up close she was drab as Boyle Heights.

I can't think of a single good reason for
anyone to move to LA . . . unless
they live in Detroit.

According to J. Edgar Hoover, Charlie
Chaplin is a communist and a pedophile.
Don't worry, Charlie, Hoover is queer.

It's The City of Angels, but the last
angel caught a Greyhound
for Pismo Beach two weeks ago.

If you live in Iowa, don't come to
LA for your vacation. It won't
make any sense to you.

Errol Flynn failed his draft physical due to heart problems, tuberculosis, venereal disease, and chronic cowardice.

LA's new Union Station is open. Now we can bring people in, separate them from their money, and ship them out much faster.

LA just got a new Police Chief, Robert Parker. They say he's an honest crime fighter. If he is, this city is in for a shock.

The "Black Dahlia"(Liz Short) got
herself killed. The way they chopped her
up, she must have really ticked somebody off.

Seen the new Capital Records tower? It's
supposed to be a stack of records on a
phonograph. Doesn't spin at 78 RPM, though.

LA's first neon sign went up in 1923. It's
at Anthony's Packard dealership and says,
"Packard." Sharp as tacks those ad folks.

They say the Egyptian Theater was inspired by King Tut 3000 years after he died. Sid Grauman got even for *The Mummy's Curse*.

I found the body at his Malibu beach house. In finer neighborhoods, laying around the house deceased is terribly gauche.

How come nothing is ever blacker than the ace of clubs?

The guy comes across as a mama's
boy but he hasn't seen his mama in years.
She's doin' twenty to life at Chino.

Mullen & Bluett is where guys who work for a
living in this town buy their clothes. It's still a
step up from the Salvation Army Thrift Store.

There are tough guys downtown, but if you
want a mug who even makes cops
nervous, go to East LA.

Call it a roscoe, heater, or gat, but if you pull it, use it. Real bad guys don't get scared until they hear it go "bang."

There are no sinister shadows in this town. There has to be some light to make shadows.

If you see a shooting on the streets of LA, don't just stand there, return fire.

San Pedro is the only town
south of Bakersfield with no illusions.

Phillip Marlowe fans hint: "Bay City" is just
Santa Monica in disguise so the cops or the
mob don't use Chandler for target practice.

If I hate LA so much, why don't I
move? That would be like a milkman
moving where there aren't any cows.

The mob and the LA cops have a code, like a set of rules. If you break them, you don't get to live anymore.

Robbing banks is amateur stuff. Pros rob the guy who just robbed the bank.

Poor Bugsy can't get no respect. They didn't even spell "Siegel" right on his toe tag at the morgue.

LA is full of dames. Ladies, on the other hand, are in short supply.

If I'd had a teacher who looked like her, I might even remember when the hell Columbus sailed the ocean blue.

I was in love once, and if I live long enough, I might forget her.

What you want to do and what you should do
are two different things. Generally,
"shoulds" help you live longer.

Her hair was a shade of blonde that
would make Mother Nature puke.

The racket coming out of the
alley sounded like the entire Spike
Jones percussion section was back there.

I've seen movie stars at their best and at their worst. There isn't much difference.

I wish somebody would pay me to look the other way when I pass a bookie joint or a whorehouse, but I don't have a badge.

If you catch a guy with his hand in your pocket, you've either got yourself a pickpocket or a politician.

I hear Joe Kennedy is our ambassador to the
UK now. That's one way to get out of
town when the law is on to you.

It says a lot about us when
Mickey Spillane sells ten times
more books than Ernest Hemingway.

Studios are making a lot of those
noir films. I'm hoping they'll make one
about me. They could call it *The Big Nap*.

This TV thing is like a movie theater in your home. If they can get it to dispense popcorn and Jujubes, they'll really have something.

Orson Welles' new film, *Citizen Kane*, is really about Willie Hearst. Welles went way too easy on him.

No matter where you're from, if you stand at Hollywood & Vine long enough you'll see someone you know, probably a bill collector.

Some guy opened a drive-through
burger joint in Baldwin Park called
In-N-Out Burger. It'll never catch on.

There's a rumor Walt Disney is tight with J.
Edgar. I already figured that because Disney's
Goofy character has to be based on Hoover.

They're gonna build a highway right through
the middle of Whitley Heights and the
rich folks up there ain't happy.

What makes writers tick?
Usually a cheap watch, but
sometimes an explosive device.

Seeing more and more good-time
girls on the Boulevard. Funny
the cops don't notice 'em.

The first Oscars were held at the Hollywood
Roosevelt back in '29. They only lasted
five minutes. L. B. Mayer had laryngitis.

Film makers are all cranking out those
psychological thrillers these days. I'll
take the Three Stooges any day.

The new Del Mar racetrack down near San
Diego was built by Bing Crosby, Pat O'Brien,
and other pony players. Doo-dah, doo-dah.

If ya don't already know what
puddles of blood on a sidewalk look
like under red neon, I hope you never do.

It was a quiet night on the
Strip . . . only three homicides.

LA's astute coroner called it suicide.
How the hell do you shoot yourself
in the back? Three times?

My pal Bogie showed me how to act
tough. He didn't tell me what to do when
I meet someone who hasn't read the script.

She was strictly a hands-off dame . . .
cute as a kitten and deadly as a sidewinder.

It was a classy crowd and I fit in like
a meatball on a banana split.

Stamps are going up to 4-cents. If postage
keeps going up, it'll be cheaper to drive
across town and deliver your own letters

Last time I saw Mabel she was on the arm of
a mobster. I just can't imagine how she
ended up dead in an East LA alley.

Bullets are like cheap hired help.
They don't much care who they kill.

She was a built and broke
blonde trying to tap some drunk
traveling salesman for bus fare to Barstow.

It was quiet on the Boulevard—so quiet
the only sound I heard was the rasp of my
own footsteps on the wet gritty sidewalk.

You could almost hear the sizzle of the
searchlight beams slicing through
the mist over Hollywood.

I heard the desolate wail of
a freight pulling out of the yard
behind Union Station. It fit my mood.

I switched off the ignition
and sat there listening to the ticking
and sighing of my cooling engine.

She was an actress. Emotions like fear
were her business, but her eyes . . .
her eyes said she wasn't acting.

Downtown LA is full of concrete
canyons. On a quiet night a gunshot
will echo through them for a long, long time.

You want to watch out for dames
in LA. Like everything else in this cockeyed
town, they are seldom what they seem.

If the guy was lookin' for trouble, he
shoulda looked in a better neighborhood.

A tiny scar on her upper lip made the
redhead seem vulnerable. She
wasn't, not in the least.

He drinks to forget something he
forgot a long time ago.

East LA? Nobody with
any sense goes near the place
in the daytime, let alone at midnight.

I knew a guy who drove race cars out at the
autodrome in Venice Beach. He said
winning didn't take speed, it took mean.

Saw that movie, *The Maltese Falcon.* Wish I
could make as much money bein' a PI as
Bogart makes pretending to be one.

Maps to movie star homes are a swell gag.
The chumps buy 'em like crazy, but how
do they know that shack is really Gable's?

Those new Studebaker cars are
perfect for guys like me. You can't tell
whether they're comin' or goin'.

Everybody makes mistakes, but when celebrities make 'em, they get expensive. That's why there are guys like me.

Ran into Spencer Tracy the other day. He was having a banana split at Pig 'N' Whistle. Some tough guy.

Was surprised to hear Bugsy got it in the back while reading a newspaper last night. I didn't think he could read.

Marijuana is the hot item with
actors now. It makes 'em stupid. That's
bad cuz most aren't too bright to start with.

Heard Rita Hayworth got picked up on a
concealed weapon charge. I just want to
know where the hell she concealed it.

They found the missing dame in
the Troc's parking lot on the Strip.
At least she picked a classy place to die.

It rained for two days last week. Hollywood flooded and ground to a halt. A desert like LA doesn't handle rain well.

Went to hear Nat "King" Cole at a classy joint. Found out he had to come and go by a rear door. No Negros allowed.

That guy Tucker who designed a new safer car went bust. Guess all his customers are already in cemeteries.

Heard Hollywood Memorial refused to bury Hattie McDaniel. Did they think the current residents would complain?

Don't know how to vote in the election. Eisenhower won the war, but Stevenson might have kept us out of it in the first place.

Some are urging Eleanor Roosevelt to run for president, but a woman on the ballot is about as likely as a Negro President.

Some actors dodged military service in WWII, but three who served bravely are Clark Gable, Jimmy Stewart, and David Niven.

Saw that new Fred MacMurray movie, *Double Indemnity*. My professional opinion: long on imagination, short on reality.

FDR signed an executive order to lock up all the Japs in the US after war broke out. That's a shame, but so was Pearl Harbor.

Northrop Aviation down in Hawthorne is building flying wings without airplanes attached. Now, that's really "winging it."

When they took the girl to Tijuana, my odds of finding her sank like a rock. Things lost down there usually stay lost.

The guy had enough bullet holes in him to make Swiss cheese jealous.

I knocked knowing full
well there was nobody inside with
enough life left in 'em to open the door.

The last time I saw Sally two state cops were
hauling her off to Tehachapi women's
prison. She didn't look happy.

Some radio actor named Jack Webb has
a detective show called *Pat Novak For
Hire*. He must have trouble saying big words.

A Bible-thumper called Billy
Graham is crusading to bring religion to
LA. Good luck with that one, fellow.

The air around here is filthy. I guess
Angelinos figure if they can't see
the air, it ain't fit to breathe.

I learn somethin' new every day. The
Wiltern Theater was named for its location at
WIL-shire & Wes-TERN. Clever . . . I guess.

The papers are full of Elizabeth Short lately. They say she went to pieces over something.

As of January, 1947, LA has KTLA, it's own TV station. Bob Hope and Pepsodent kicked things off from Paramount Studios.

The cops already know who killed Bugsy. So do I. All I'll say is it was done FOR the Lansky mob, but not BY them. No big deal.

Sunset Gardens veteran housing has a sign saying, "This tract is exclusive and restricted." Good thing for us the Army wasn't as picky.

According to the 1950 census LA's population is 1,970,358, making us the fourth largest city in the country. Swell.

Truman fired General MacArthur the other day, calling him a "dumb son of a bitch." Is that any way for a US President to talk?

Why should I pay to see dark mysteries in a theater when I can see 'em for free right outside on Hollywood Boulevard?

I hear Betty Grable is the most popular actress for 1949, and she doesn't even have to blow her own horn. Don't get it? Never mind.

I guess I was about ten when I first saw the island. That was the beginning of a lifelong love affair with Catalina.

What's with these people who
insist on saying Los An-ga-lees?

Battle of LA: The sky was full of tracer
bullets, but the Navy says no Jap planes, so
we must've been shootin' at Martians.

Drove out the strip the other night to
see what's new. They've got
some new neon, but the same old sin.

East LA is up in arms: Chief Davis' "Gun
Squad" blasted a couple of prominent
citizens and actually shot some bad guys.

I understand many folks in
other places think LA is no place
for decent people to live. They're right.

Seems doctors knew FDR had cancer and
heart disease before last year's election.
Now his wife is running the country.

Politicians are fooling with Daylight Savings Time again. I don't know why. Most of them aren't bright enough to tell time anyway.

This time of year we get the hot Santa Ana winds. They make everyone sweaty and mean . . . especially mean.

The only way to solve LA's Mexican problem is give the place back to them.

In pueblo times, there was one street in LA to avoid if you valued your life: "Calle de los Negros." Today the list is much longer.

Have no fear, there will always be a Los Angeles. There is no way they will ever get rid of all that concrete.

Dark alleys? LA is lousy with 'em. In fact, I don't know of any LA alleys that aren't dark.

LA is like no other city in the world. That is something for which the world should be extremely grateful.

How do you get a big studio acting contract? By being in the right place at the wrong time.

Broderick Crawford won the Best Actor Oscar the other night. It was good to see a tough guy win for a change.

If folks who read movie fan magazines saw
what really goes on here, they'd stick
to *National Geographic*.

Gene Autry is leading the Santa Claus Parade
again this year, so you better watch out, you
better not cry, and you better not pout!

Came across Bob Cummings' real name:
Charles Clarence Robert Orville Cummings.
No wonder he's always bombed on drugs.

Is Robert Benchley throwing his annual holiday bash at the Garden again this year? It gives new meaning to "Christmas spirits."

Even the working girls on
the Strip have the holiday spirit.
I saw one wearing a Santa hat today.

When the Japs bombed Pearl Harbor, they committed hara-kiri.

LA's night music . . . the rattle of the red cars
for folks going somewhere and sirens
for those who are already there.

I remember the day I met Maggie Brown.
She arrived in my office with ten cents for
carfare and ten grand worth of blues.

I wanted to hear some jazz, so
I went to Dunbar's lounge. Sure, it's
a Negro joint, so what? The jazz is great.

A guy I know—call him Jake—says the San Fernando Valley is stealing our water. That seems fair since we stole it in the first place.

The cops went lookin' for Ben Siegel the other day. They found him hiding in his attic. Real smart, Bugsy.

Heard they found a dead mob guy in Lake Hollywood. Come on, guys, we have to drink that water.

The nights in Hollywood are longer
than they are anywhere else.

If Lucky Luciano and Frank
Nitti ever get bumped off, most of the
cops in LA are gonna be back to eatin' beans.

When a 38 slug passes within inches of your
ear, it makes whirring sound. By the time
you hear the sound, it's too late to duck.

I don't exactly know how much blood is in the
human body, but I'm sure this guy
was several quarts low.

Fashion tip. If you're going out to
get shot, don't wear a white dinner jacket.

These days Packards are gangster cars.
Nobody who is legit drives one.

They say that new movie, *Sunset Boulevard*,
will be a classic someday. Could be.
It's just as sleazy as the street it's named for.

Sepulveda Boulevard is a long street. It starts
in the Valley and ends in Long Beach. For
Mitzi Delgado, it was a 43 mile drive to hell.

Helped a friend move yesterday. He was
one of the last honest cops in this
town. His new address is Forest Lawn.

They say there are good girls and there are
nice girls. She was a good girl until
the mob made her a nice girl.

If you want to catch bad guys,
you have to hang out in the bad part of
town. That's why there aren't any cops there.

Her heart was blacker than
the La Brea tar pits.

Some tough guys kill for money; this
character kills for the pure joy of it.

Broadway runs right through
the heart of Chinatown, where you
can get chop suey or a knife in the back.

There are crooked cops just about
everywhere, but out in Santa Monica
they've made it into an art form.

At the risk of disillusioning the tourists
who flock to our beaches, the pretty white
seagulls are just flying rats, only not as picky.

Tough guy actor George Raft had
a knife pulled on him in a bar out on the
Strip. Word is he wet his pants.

A word to guys who'd like to put the slug
on Frank Sinatra: It can be done, but
it's likely to be the last thing you ever do.

Business Opportunity: Peddle suspenders to
all the politicians who keep getting
caught with their pants down.

LA is sort of like the British
Empire, only in reverse. The sun
never rises in some parts of Los Angeles.

Angelinos have discovered the word "smog."
Funny thing is, both the smog and the
word have been around since the 1880s.

Word is Cary Grant and Randolph Scott are more than pals. Sorry girls.

Film stars are just like us. They put their pants on one leg at a time . . . when they can find their pants.

Hollywood Boulevard is getting trashier every day. It is so bad the pigeons have moved to Melrose Avenue.

The Destroyer USS Thompson was just decommissioned. So What? Film fans know the ship better as the USS Caine.

Lucky Luciano is a very religious guy. He even has his own Golden Rule: "Do unto others before they do unto him."

Good Christian folks seem to avoid LA. I can't imagine why. Hell, we have Aimee Semple McPherson and Billy Graham.

The LA River is a war between Mother Nature and man. So far Mother Nature is winning.

Seems we have a new generation of people in this country who are unfamiliar with the words "please" and "thank you."

Heed those "no trespassing" signs in Beverley Hills. Trespass there and a property owner can legally shoot you dead.

The forecourt of Sid Grauman's Egyptian Theater was plastered with anti-Semitic signs last night. Come on, people.

The Hollywood C of C says crime on the Boulevard is scaring tourists away. At last, something positive about crime!

Is the Doheney mansion in Beverly Hills really haunted? Some say if ghosts drove cars they'd need valet parking up there.

From Angels Flight at the top of Bunker Hill, you can see the entire city. Can't see any Angels, though. They all left town long ago.

They're demolishing the Broadway Tunnel to make way for Highway 101. Where the hell is the mob gonna stash bodies now?

The trick to shooting someone is don't miss.

What you've got in L A is flat and lots
of it. When it rains a little, the water has
no place to go so it sits around and floods.

Night is the best time in this city.
The evil is still there, but it's harder
to see it watching you.

Tip: The muzzle velocity of a .38 caliber slug
is 1,100 feet/second. Fifty feet away,
you've got 45/100ths of a second to duck.

A customer at Barney's called him on his
"FAGOTS STAY OUT" sign behind the bar.
They told him he misspelled "faggots."

Some gal once told me I must be
terribly brave to be a private eye. I guess
"brave" is a synonym for "incredibly stupid."

LA is nothing more than a miserable desert
with a stinking swamp in the middle of
it, but the suckers keep coming.

Today's Hollywood is mostly the invention of land developer Hobart Whitley. Now you know who to blame.

The guy who comes up with a bulletproof fedora is gonna make a bundle.

They say L. B. Mayer was in a love triangle with Jeanette MacDonald and Nelson Eddy. I don't buy it. Who could love a rat like Mayer?

Why do stars live such libertine lives? They've got nothing else to do with all their money and the studios have to bail them out.

Studio people tell me folks in the Midwest are the biggest film fans. Why good God fearing folks would go to movies is beyond me.

Once she was drop dead gorgeous.
Now you can skip the "gorgeous" part.

You know you need a new wardrobe
when a guy at Pink's offers to buy you a
hotdog because you look down on your luck.

There isn't an ambulance driver in LA
who doesn't know his way to the
downtown Barclay Hotel.

Word is Selznick fired George Cukor as
director of *Gone With the Wind* because
Gable wouldn't work with a homosexual.

The cops found her wandering along
Sunset in a daze with my card in
her purse. I have all the luck.

Thought I might buy myself
some life insurance. The agent
asked what I do. He's still laughing.

Met a client downtown at the Biltmore
Hotel. That joint is like a gilded
cage looking for a bird.

If bad guys were really as stupid as they are on that Gang Busters radio show, there wouldn't be any gangs left to bust.

A psychiatrist told me people aren't afraid of the dark, they just fear what they can't see in the dark. Now, why didn't think of that?

Why do they make so many noir films? Cost. Studios shoot second string talent overacting in the dark on cheap black and white film.

When papers are short on news, they drag out poor Elizabeth Short again. The Black Dahlia is dead and the cops ain't talkin', so forget it.

The *Examiner's* Louella Parsons always has high praise a certain blonde actress with the initials MD? Why do you suppose that is?

Why don't LA cops like private investigators? Because we don't get paid to look the other way.

I'm the guy ritzy joints call when they need a drunk actor removed from the premises. I don't get extra if they puke in my car.

There's a war goin' on in China
and another one in Europe. Wanna
bet which one we get suckered into first?

FDR needs to reign Eleanor in. With all her columns and radio shows she gets more attention than him. Or maybe that's the idea.

How long does it take to drink yourself to death? According to a friend at Universal Studios it took John Barrymore ten years.

Lewis Stone, died of a heart attack while chasing kids who threw rocks at his home. Somebody should stone the kids' parents.

Cagney told Jack Warner he was sick of guns and beating up women. Warner asked Cagney if he was sick of his salary, too.

Word is L. B. Mayer and B. P. Schulberg hate
each other. That's the most sense either
of them has ever shown.

Take in a show at the Vogue Theater
on the Boulevard and you might see more
than a movie. They claim the joint is haunted.

A hot dog joint, Tail O' The Pup, just opened
on San Vincente. The joint is shaped like a
hot dog. I was sure you'd want to know that.

One of Jack Warner's more astute observations: "You know Flynn, he's either got to be fighting or f*cking."

Mickey Cohen's enforcer, Johnny Stompanato, is dead. Not knowing who killed him should not spoil the celebration.

Why does property in LA cost so much? Will Rogers figured that one out: "There is only so much land and they aren't making any more."

"A woman is like a tea bag. You can't tell how strong she is until you put her in hot water." So says quipster Eleanor Roosevelt.

The Flamingo will open in Vegas Christmas, 1946. Good thing Bugsy's Jewish because he won't see Christmas, 1947.

Swim where you like: Ethel Prioleau, a Negro woman, sued the city of LA to end segregation of city pools. She won.

LA bought a landing strip way out in the bean fields of Westchester to use as a municipal airport. How convenient.

LA's new airport will be named for W. Mines, the real estate sharpie who suckered the city into buying the property.

While on the *Revolver* caper, I heard Jack Warner tell producer Hal Wallis: "I don't want it good, I want it tomorrow!"

I drove the kid to the bus depot and gave her twenty for a ticket home. It was my good deed for the day. I don't think she saw it that way.

I sat at a front table and counted fly specks on the window while I ate my chili.

I'm hearing talk about more signals on the Strip. There's no traffic out there, so we must need more seagull roosts.

The guy on the floor had a lot
of Latin blood in him once, but
most of it was in the carpet now.

Tourists come to Tinsel Town expecting to
see movie stars walking down the street.
Movie stars don't *walk* anywhere.

Most of Hollywood's glamor
is neon. Switch off the power
and all you've got is darkness.

The county road gang is digging up Sunset
west of La Cienega again. There's gotta
be gold under there somewhere.

LA lousy is with palm trees.
They don't give any shade, so they
plant 'em in a desert. Makes a lot of sense.

The east coast mobs are so thick in LA the
mugs are trippin' over each other.

You can buy anything at the LA Produce
Market from peppercress to a $50 murder.

LA has officially had a "Chinatown" since
1938. It's a good place to get thousand-
year-old eggs or a knife in the back.

Coroners will tell you a broken
heart is not a legit cause of death, but
that's what killed her, sure as anything.

Judging by the pile of cigarette butts, he sat
there for some time before working up
the nerve to blow his brains out.

Her roommate said Elaine didn't
wake up screaming like most nights.
That was because her nightmare came true.

He had pale blue eyes that chilled you to the
bone with one look. Fortunately, they
won't be doing anymore looking.

Maybe he didn't cheat the syndicate, but it
looked like he had, and that was
enough to get him killed.

By daylight the railyard is in constant motion.
After dark it is huge looming shapes
that clatter and clank when the wind blows.

I like to go up to Mullholland at night and
look at the lights in the basin. Sometimes
I imagine it was all built by Lionel.

They're everywhere—street-corner zealots crying for repentance. "Save your soul, the judgement day is coming!" Amen, brother.

The car in my rearview was a tail. I knew it because its right headlight was off kilter. Little things can save your life.

A lot of things can kill you, even love. It's what killed the pretty blonde on the bed in room 423. She loved the wrong guy.

Science is wrong. Time is not constant. When you are waiting for something it crawls or flies depending on what you're waiting for.

There's an expression folks get on their face at the moment of a violent death. It's kind of a grimace. Once you see it, you don't forget it.

You didn't have to be Dr. Kildare to know the guy was dead. The first clue was a throat problem. It was slit from ear to ear.

I drove into Malibu Canyon searching for a clue, but the clue found me. I rounded a bend and a big 45 slug shattered my windshield.

Since I don't have Lamont Cranston's power to cloud men's minds, I watched from behind a stinking garbage can.

The stagnant canals of Venice were the bad idea of Abbot Kinney, but the mob finds them convenient for dumping bodies.

Sam Spade has been played by everyone from Bogart to Eddie Robinson. They'd probably get Gabby Hayes to play me.

The Acme mail-order detective course says the first step is look for clues, but I already had clues. What I didn't have was a crime.

I was in a bad spot. I knew who killed the guy, but if I let on I knew, it would be the end of Johnny Spicer.

Hoodlums have saps. If you can't afford one, make a sap with a sock and ball bearings. Just make sure there aren't any holes in the sock.

I've never seen it written anywhere that hoods have to be snappy dressers, but they always are. You can spot 'em a mile away.

When something or someone disappears, they call me. I usually find what's missing . . . unless it doesn't want to be found.

Then the rain came and my view of the
Strip through my windshield became a
smeary mess of dust turning to mud.

The H and two Os were missing, along
with parts of the Ls. HOLLYWOODLAND
had seen better days. So had I.

I bypassed the Frolic Room
and drove down to The Blue Room
on Melrose. I wasn't in a frolicking mood.

While I was trying to clear the spider webs
out of my brain, the spider showed up
and conked me on the noggin again.

The most useless thing in the
world is the revolver you left in your
desk when you went out to catch the bad guy.

The dough Hollywood folks spend on snazzy
Dueseys, Packards, and Caddys would
buy three Red Car trolley systems.

He was a veteran of the LAPD—a sergeant no less—and he was paying far more attention to me than I was worth.

The first thing I noticed about her were her rundown shoes . . . well, the first thing after the bullet hole in her temple.

He was one of those guys who always whine about how life dealt 'em a lousy hand. With three thirty-eight slugs in him, maybe it did.

Gary Cooper and I aren't pals, but I know him well enough not to let the bum near my daughter . . . if I had a daughter.

Party sounds drifted through my office window. I poured another shot and imagined I was one of the madcap merrymakers.

They loaded Elinor Ince into an ambulance in front of the Château Élysée. Even after two decades she still makes W. R. nervous.

He drank beyond excess.
He drank all the way to oblivion.

The 1940 census says 1.5 million people live within LA's 500 square miles. That's room for a lot of crime and lots of folks to commit it.

I noticed some working girls out on the Strip giving friendly waves to a passing sheriff's cruiser. Maybe they attend the same church.

I read there are nearly a million cars in LA.
Today they are all tan Fords because I'm
looking for a guy in a tan Ford.

Sure, I know lots of guys in LA, but if I know
'em, chances are you don't want to.

The 1940 census says 40% of the people in
California live in LA County.
No wonder I can never find a parking place.

Boyle Heights is the sort of neighborhood where you walk a little faster after dark . . . actually, a lot faster.

They put up new streetlights in Hollywood. The pigeons have taken to them, which discourages leaning on lampposts.

The streetlamp behind me cast my shadow a long way into the alley. Whoever was back there sure as hell knew I was coming.

I trotted over to take a look for survivors in
the wrecked cars. Then dripping gasoline
lit and I didn't need to go any closer.

I wasn't gonna tell him he was wrong. He was
one of those guys who is big enough to be
right no matter how wrong they are.

I don't care what cops say, you never get
used to dead bodies. You just learn
to look in another direction a little harder.

The pretty redhead's ID said she was from
Nebraska. If she'd stayed in Nebraska,
she might still be a living pretty redhead.

For a real thrill, visit the La Brea tar pits after
dark. I'd swear some of those saber-
tooth tigers are still movin' around out there.

There is little angelic influence in this town
named for angels. There are a few angels
here, though. They are the ones who care.

She didn't come here to be a waitress. The diner job was just until she got her big break. I tipped her a buck and wished her luck.

On my way back from Beverly Hills, I swung into Barney's Beanery. It was a chili and Pabst Blue Ribbon kind of day.

Not only are our boys fighting Japs in the Pacific, they're also fighting Pachuco zoot suiters at Chavez Ravine.

Actors are ideal blackmail targets because the studios always pay off. This time Jack Warner said "no." Jane B no longer has a film career.

My new client stepped on the wrong toes and the cops were framing her for murder. At least that was her story.

Wild fires burn off plants that hold the topsoil in place. That means next winter your uphill neighbor's house will be in your backyard.

Pulp writers who talk about "the smell of cordite" are behind the times. Most ammo makers stopped using cordite after WWI.

Since WWII ended Gilmore has been trying something new: Gas-A-Teria self-service gasoline stations. Ain't gonna work.

A young screenwriter came in wanting to know about private cops. I can't wait to see what he makes of the hogwash I gave him.

The LA River is more than 40 miles of concrete from start to end. You could call it a fishy freeway . . . if there were any fish.

The Colorado Street bridge to oblivion: More than a hundred folks have taken the 150-foot dive into Arroyo Seco since 1913.

Despite Columbia Pictures being there, Sunset and Gower is still known as "poverty row." Harry Cohn doesn't seem to mind.

Christmas is coming to Hollywood. There's fake holly in every shop window and a phony Santa on every corner. It's all very festive.

Someday we'll all wake up and find out LA was never really here. That's how nightmares work.

Drifters blow into town, but they don't stay. To survive in LA you need street savvy they don't teach anywhere else.

They don't dare drive all the corruption out of LA. If they did, there wouldn't be anybody left to run the city.

If there was a lot of gold in the world, it wouldn't be worth a plug nickel. In this town the same goes for people.

At night Hollywood Boulevard becomes a neon nightmare—a nightmare some folks never wake up from.

When the breeze is just right I can smell
the kitchen at the Hollywood Hotel across
Highland. They're having fish tonight.

No amount of flashy neon could make the
joint anything but what it was—a tourist
trap hustling watered-down booze.

Raymond Chandler died the other
day. Phillip Marlowe and I will miss him.
(March 26, 1959)

MEET H. P. OLIVER

H. P. Oliver began his career with a degree in journalism from San Jose State University and spent the next twenty-some years writing award-winning entertainment and educational media. Now he applies his creativity and imagination to writing historical mysteries.

About mystery writing, Oliver says, "To be truly engrossing, a mystery needs a little meat on its bones—something more than just figuring out who did the evil deed.

Taking a story back in time or even basing it on actual historical events is a great way to endow a good yarn with even more color and depth. Historical periods and locations give writers an opportunity to take readers where they've never been before."

H. P. Oliver lives in northern California and spends much of his time working on projects throughout the western states. In addition to his love of history, Oliver's interests range from vintage film to restoring classic cars.

For information about H. P. Oliver's books, including synopses, previews, video trailers, and purchase links, visit his fan site at www.HPOliver.com, where you will also find illustrated history articles and other fascinating features. Plan to stay a while, there's a lot to see and do.

BOOKS BY H. P. OLIVER

◆ CLASSIC MYSTERIES IN HISTORY ◆

THE TRUTH BE TOLD
(E-Book)

AND THE ANGELS SING
(E-Book)

SILENTS!
(E-Book & Paperback)

WINGING IT
(E-Book & Paperback)

ESTELLE
(E-Book & Paperback)

GOODNIGHT, SAN FRANCISCO
(E-Book & Paperback)

SO LONG, L A
(E-Book & Paperback)

◆ JOHNNY SPICER CAPERS ◆

JOHNNY SPICER: THE FIRST CAPERS
(E-Book)

PACIFICA
(E-Book & Paperback)

REVOLVER
(E-Book & Paperback)

TEMBO
(E-Book & Paperback)

S. N. A. F. U.
(E-Book & Paperback)

PAYBACK
(E-Book & Paperback)

H. P. Oliver's books are available at Amazon.com